The Tortoise Fair

Written and Illustrated by
John Patience

DERRYDALE BOOKS
New York
© Fern Hollow Productions Ltd.
Peter Haddock Ltd., U.K.
This 1984 edition is published by Derrydale Books,
distributed by Crown Publishers, Inc.
Printed in Italy
ISBN 0-517-457970
hgfedcba

Early one morning an old tortoise appeared in Fern Hollow. He was dressed like a gypsy and was pasting up posters. Tugger and Monty read the posters with great excitement: "The Tortoise Fair. Coming to Fern Hollow tomorrow." Monty and Tugger loved fairs and the Tortoise himself was a very interesting animal. He said his name was Pablo and he told them stories about all the wonderful places he had visited. "Like all tortoises," he said, "I take my house around with me. Yes indeed, it's a traveling life for me. A gypsy life in a painted caravan."

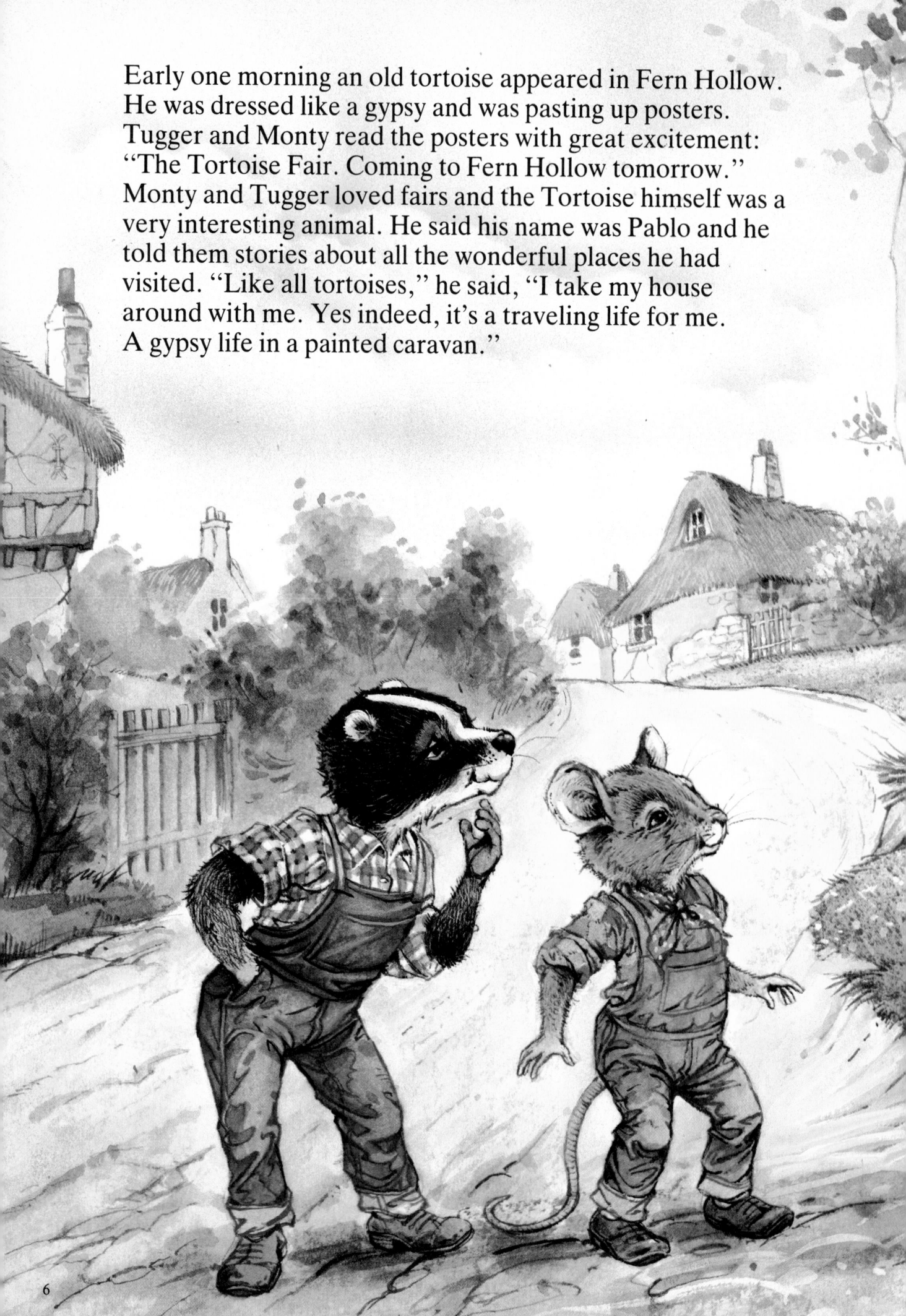

This book belongs to:

....

The next day Monty and Tugger went to the fair. It had been put up in Farmer Bramble's (Tugger's father's) field. All the Fern Hollow animals were there and everyone was having fun. There were merry-go-rounds, coconut tosses and lots of other things besides. Tugger won a goldfish and Monty won a coconut. As evening came, everyone began to drift off home. "Listen," whispered Tugger. "The fair leaves here tomorrow morning. Meet me here then and we'll go with them!"

The sun had just risen and a thick dew was sparkling on the grass. Tugger had hidden himself behind a tree near Pablo's caravan. Suddenly, someone tapped him on his shoulder. "Don't worry, it's only me," whispered Monty. "You gave me the fright of my life," replied Tugger.
It was quite likely that the tortoises wouldn't want to take Monty and Tugger with them so the friends decided that they would stow themselves away. As they crept into Pablo's caravan the old tortoise was still fast asleep. Monty pointed to a large wicker basket. "We'll hide in there," he whispered.

Before long, the fairground folk began to wake up. Then
there was a lot of noisy activity as the merry-go-rounds and
sideshows were packed away, and the horses were hitched up
to the caravans. At last they were all ready to leave. "Giddy
up, Topper," shouted Pablo. Then Monty and Tugger felt
the caravan jolt and move off.

The caravan was just crossing the railroad bridge when the
Fern Hollow express came down the line. Suddenly, Mr.
Rusty the engine driver sounded the whistle. Toot, toot,
toot, toot! The noise terrified Topper, he whinnied, reared
up and bolted off down the road with the caravan rattling
along wildly behind him.

13

Topper galloped on through the village, scattering the Fern Hollow animals before him like leaves in the wind. No one tried to stop the runaway horse, until P.C. Hoppit, who was riding along on his bicycle, saw it charging towards him. "Stop in the name of the law," he cried. But the next moment the brave policeman was knocked off his bicycle and found himself sitting, dusty and dazed, by the roadside.

Later that day, Mr. and Mrs. Tuttlebee noticed that Monty was missing and went to see P.C. Hoppit. When they arrived at the police station they found that Farmer Bramble and his

wife were also there. It seemed that Tugger was missing too. "The tortoises must have kidnapped them," deduced P.C. Hoppit. "They were certainly in a hurry to leave. We'd better get after them." "Come on, then," cried Farmer Bramble. "I've got the tractor outside. You can all ride in the trailer. We'll track the villains down or my name's not Barnaby Bramble!"

Meanwhile, Pablo had managed to get Topper under control and the traveling fairground was now on its way to the next village. In the wicker basket, Tugger's nose had begun to itch. Suddenly he sneezed, ATCHOOOO!

Pablo almost jumped out of his shell. The two stowaways had given themselves away, but fortunately for them, the old tortoise was very understanding "Well, I'll have to take you back home," he chuckled. "But it's getting late and I expect you're hungry. You can have supper with us first." Soon Monty and Tugger were sitting round the campfire, eating stew and singing songs to the music of Pablo's accordion.

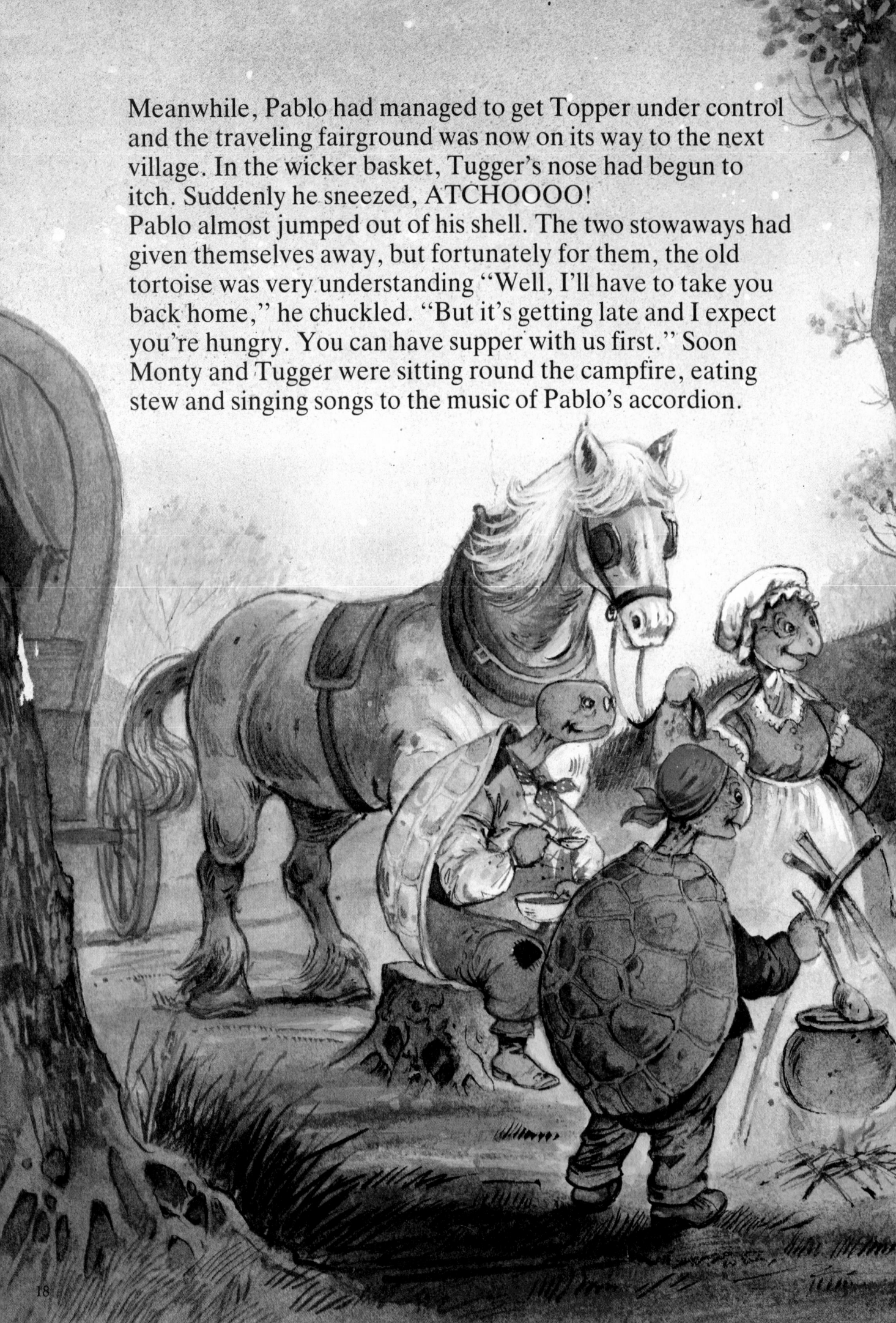

The stew had all been eaten and Pablo was preparing to turn back to Fern Hollow, when Farmer Bramble drove up on his tractor. P.C. Hoppit was quite ready to arrest every one of the tortoises for kidnapping, but Monty and Tugger quickly explained what had happened. "Well," said Farmer Bramble, as he drove the tractor and trailer home. "You two have certainly had an adventure, haven't you?" But there was no reply from Monty or Tugger because they had both fallen fast asleep.

Fern Hollow

MR CHIPS'S HOUSE

MR WILLOWBANK'S
COBBLER'S SHOP

THE JOLLY VOLE
HOTEL

MR CROAKER'S WATERMILL

STRIPEY'S HOUSE

SCHOOL

RIVER FERNY

MR ACORN'S
BAKERY

MR RUSTY'S HOUSE

MR PRICKLES'S HOUSE

POST OFFICE

BORIS BLINKS'S
BOOKSHOP

MR TWINKLE'S
HOUSE

MR TUTTLEEBEE'S
SHOP

MR THIMBLE'S
TAILORS SHOP

WINDYWOOD